Another Year of Plumdog

ALSO BY EMMA CHICHESTER CLARK

Plumdog
The Plumdog Path to Perfection

PLUMDOG TITLES FOR CHILDREN

Love is My Favourite Thing!
Plenty of Love to Go Round

Another Year of Plumdog

Emma Chichester Clark

JONATHAN CAPE
LONDON

For
all my friends
and relations
and acquaintances
far and wide,
and anyone else
who would like
a dedication,
or who has never
had one.

Friday 1st January

New year! New house! New life!

New year resolutions:
1. Catch a fox.
2. Catch a cat (not Gracie).
3. Stay here.

Monday 4th January

Today I modelled sofas and armchairs and Emma took photographs

to see which ones suited me best.

Then Emma modelled clothes and I waited and waited, listening to the expletives, and then we went home without any new clothes or new sofas or new armchairs, and we both felt much better.

Sat 9th January

Peg and I had to pose
for the Suffolk Ladies
Amateur Camera Club for
hours. It's just one of the
burdens of being
Objects of Beauty.

Sunday 10th January

We went for a walk with a lot of tall, thin people.
They tottered along incredibly slowly because they were all talking, non-stop.

Even my daddy was there, and he was keeping up really well.

It was probably the longest walk he's ever been on.

But just as I was thinking how proud of him I was...

... he flagged down a nice man from the National Trust and asked him to drive him home.

Tuesday 12th January

I really like Claudia. I've known her all my life, but I never know if she really likes me quite as much.

It's probably because she never wants me to kiss her.

It makes her even more fascinating and enigmatic.

It was Grandpa's birthday. I promised
I wouldn't make another joke about his
age in dog years but it's 602, I think.
Fia gave him a little tiny birthday cake.
It's Liffey and my birthday tomorrow.—
I'm really hoping our cake won't be
carrot and it will be a LOT bigger.

Sunday 17th January

It was mine and Liffey's birthday yesterday so our brother, Alfie, and our half-brother, Barney, and our long-lost sister, Greta came to tea.

After we'd opened all our presents and eaten the cake we all wanted to fight and bite each other but we weren't allowed to, so we just glared at each other and growled gruesomely - all except Barney who didn't know where to look.
Emma and Fia said it was a pity we were so inhospitable.

Sometimes Emma finds a nice stick.

I never let her keep it.

Once it's mine - it's mine, no matter how nicely she asks or how bossy she is. It's mine.

She chases, pathetically slow...

she creeps, but I have eyes and ears.

It's mine! It's mine!

Then she finds another stick. That will soon be mine too.

Saturday 23rd January

Emma took me with her to the chiropractor, even though dogs aren't allowed in. She put me in a bag because she thought no one would notice me.

It was so embarrassing.

It was fine in the cubicle with Amy She didn't mind.

But when we went out through reception we were both blushing from head to tail.

Monday 25th January

I did telepathy with Rocket today. He said "Hello Plum," and I said "Hello Rocket." Then he said "I can see you," and I said "I can see you too." Then we ran out of things to say.

Wednesday 27th January

Emma said it was time for some Home Grooming. She said it was ESSENTIAL because, in her words, I was a "STINK BOMB."

So no area was left untouched or un-interfered with.

I finally lost it when she came at me with the hairbrush.

After all – I LIKED the stink bomb smell. I had searched it out. I had chosen it. I had gone to a great deal of trouble to spread it evenly. Now I'll just have to do it all over again.

Tuesday, 28th January

I've been suspicious for a few days because Emma has been writing lists and tidying things, so I wasn't really surprised when I caught her packing a suitcase. But where is she going, and will she ever come back?

Wednesday 3rd February

Emma and my daddy were both away all week, I don't know where but they were not here anywhere. Weezie was here instead. Emma doesn't know what we did so she can't draw the pictures. She just has to imagine and draw what I tell her.

Maybe it was like this ← I say.

Or, maybe it was like this →

Maybe I just won't tell her.

Friday 5th February

When Emma was unpacking her suitcase she said, "Plummee! I've got a lovely present for you!" Things were looking up, I thought.

I forgot that her idea of a lovely present was different to mine.

My attempt to escape was pointless.

"It fits!" she shrieked. She had a look of pure happiness on her poor old face, and who am I to deny her that?

Sunday 7th February

If anyone makes a rude noise or an awful smell in our house they always say "Oh, Plum!" It's so unfair and I'm fed up with it. It is more than irksome and I don't suppose that I'm the only dog who has to put up with it. So, when I found some ancient, abandoned fish and chips in the park and ate them before Emma could stop me — well... later on that evening... I can only say they had it coming to them: I EXCELLED myself, and all the cries of "Oh, Plum!" were entirely justified.

Wednesday 10th February

Today Emma was looking after Grandpa, Blind Maudie, and me, because we are all poorly, poorly things. Roll on Spring.

Friday 12th February

Day 1

I think Emma has finally cracked. For the last three days she has been collecting my very own private poo...

Day 2

...and putting it in a special pot. It might be because of me being ill, but I'm much better now...

Day 3

...or maybe she's starting a poo museum?

Saturday 13th February

I wonder when Emma will admit that my new coat is a bit too BIG.

It's like a wind-tunnel.

I hope she'll notice before I'm caught in an updraught.

air-borne in the bluster.

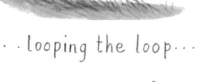

··looping the loop···

·· wafting a-w-a-a-a-y .

Wednesday 17th February

Yesterday, Love came knocking at my door:

Love, in the shape of the small, but perfectly-formed Rocket.

This time we just took up where we left off.

I've learnt that life is too short for recriminations.

Why waste time haranguing a bloke who's commitment phobic—

— when you can simply and gloriously do this?

Saturday 20th February. We drove to Suffolk for the weekend. My daddy sang along with Bob Dylan for 2½ hours. It was bracing.

Suffolk is new country for him but he is embracing it positively. Claudia came and embraced it too. The wind and sea were extremely bracing. On the way home Emma and Claudia wittered on while my daddy and I embraced and slept all the way. Today I have embraced a new word. The more I write it - the odder it looks.

Thurs. 25th February   A beautiful day - Spring in the air, buds budding and birds singing. It was a day for springing and singing - but - "Did you notice?" asked Esther. Of course I did. I hadn't been able to think about anything else: Emma and Trisha didn't buy any croissants. Croissants weren't mentioned at all. They seemed to have made a decision without consulting US...

Friday 26th February

So much for sharing. Esther may be my best friend but sometimes she is a thug. Otherwise, it was a beautiful day.

Saturday 27th February

Our friend Claudia has a new dog called Maddy.

Liffey and I were a bit disappointed that she felt she needed another dog in her life as well as us — especially one who is so bouncy and much too friendly. Maddy thinks everything is fun, fun, fun. Well, we had a word with her. Now she knows we are NOT quite as sweet and fun as we look.

I was really excited about going to supper with my relations...

... except I forgot that Clara would be there. Liffey, my sister, says I am silly to mind about her. It's not that I won't be fond of her, one day. I just don't understand about her being so big and bouncy now.
Luckily, my family understand about me.

They don't say I'm silly, Liffey.

Thursday 4th March

There are a lot of opportunities for between meal snacking in our park.

Despite the numerous bins people drop food everywhere

and it all looks delicious to me. But nowadays, ever since I was ill, Emma is ON MY CASE.

She says even an innocent French fried potato is a death trap and I realise that I now live in a Nanny State with my very own super-caring Prophet of Doom.

Tuesday 8th March

I am not normally allowed to stand on the kitchen table but today I was put there.

Emma said it was time to "do something about my hair."
She kept saying I was "sooo good for keeping still..."

Frankly, being good had nothing to do with it. The woman was wielding a pair of scissors and in my view—some are born with certain skills and others—probably not.

When she'd finished she said, "Oh, Plummie! You look like a spring lamb!"
"Great!" I thought. "Just the look I was hoping for."

Thursday 10th March

For a change, we went to Kensington Gardens. I was conceived there. I was hoping I might bump into my real father, but so far, I never have.

Monday 14th March

Spring is in the air
and in my hair.

The look is chic,
jaunty, gamine,

rather like
Audrey Hepburn,
I think.

My friend on Twitter,
Pom Pom Whippet,
sent me this
divine
scarf.

It is the essence
of MOI and the
essential ornament
of the season.

Wednesday 16th March

A Poem

Esther, Tosca, and me
Stood under the cherry tree
It was pink all around,
In the sky, on the ground-
The prettiest tree I could see.
by Plum.

Friday 18th March

I had a traumatic time in the square, beginning with the ritual humilation that I have to endure from the rotund chihuahuas in high-pitched Chinese. They do it to me every time and I never know what to say. Then the oldest dog in Britain sniffed my bottom for an unreasonably long period of time and I didn't know what to say to him either. Meanwhile his mate fixed me in an intimidating Eye to Eye and the chihuahuas giggled like schoolgirls. I thought up lots of Things to Say on the way home. I always seem to think of brilliant things much too late to say them.

Sunday 20th March

Emma took me to another Blue Kangaroo event. I was looking forward to it a lot, until I remembered I'd have to be quiet and listen to those stories AGAIN,

and I'd just begun to groan quietly with boredom when suddenly, a giant Blue Kangaroo came out of a cupboard! It was quite a shock, but also a perfect opportunity —

so I said "Watch out, you over-sized, puffed-up blue marsupial! When my book comes out, that stage will be MINE, all mine!" He didn't even flinch.

<u>Monday 21st March</u> Liffey came to stay with us in Suffolk. There are hundreds of dogs there and she was impressed by the huge number of friends I have. She introduced herself saying, "I'm Plum's sister!" and everyone was very polite and friendly.

But then I heard her say to Peg, "Plum is so popular, isn't she?" And Peg replied, "Liffey dear, nobody has any idea who she is." So I suppose I'll never hear the end of it now.

Thursday 24th March

We went for a walk to my favourite place with Emma's Old Flame. He and I have a quickness of sympathy that is rare, even between a dog and a man. We also share a love of water and boats, so I found a boat and hoped he'd take me sailing, but he just looked at me. He simply didn't seem to understand at all.

Saturday 26th March

I was everybody's favourite on Thursday evening but then Maddie arrived, and by Sunday, everything had changed. It was a bit of an unfortunate misunderstanding.

Maddy didn't understand that everything in my house was mine - no matter how often I told her.

Emma called me "a little black horror", and I ended up in the garden, watching Maddy making herself quite at home.

Monday 28th March

Sometimes I just bask. I let my mind go free. I let everything go. I am one with the sun. I am light. I am nothing. I am the sun. I am. I am not. I am asleep.

Wednesday 30ᵗʰ March

In Kensington Gardens again. The Queen was perfectly happy to have me in her pond so I don't know why Emma got so stroppy.

Friday 1st April

Yesterday I hurt my leg.

I don't know how I did it, but now I have a limp.

Emma says to try not to think about it...

...but I can't stop.

I can't stop thinking about it all the time.

Saturday 2nd April

We went to stay with Grandpa because Caroline and Maudie were away. I absolutely adore Grandpa, and he kept saying what a nice dog I was.

I slept in Maudie's bed,

and when we went for a walk I pretended I belonged to Grandpa, but...

... then Caroline and Maudie came home, and, I'm very ashamed to say I was extremely rude to Maudie, which was unforgivable, as she is completely blind these days. I sort of forgot it was her house. She was too scared to come in. Poor Maudie.

Everyone was upset. Even me. Especially because Grandpa saw— and now I'm afraid he might have gone off me.

Sunday 3rd April

We woke up to one of those days - a nothing day, dreary, dull, depressing, dreadful, and Emma said she was getting a cold.

The only answer to days like this came to us both in a moment of perfect symbiosis—

— favourite dental chew for me, packet of Minstrels for Emma.

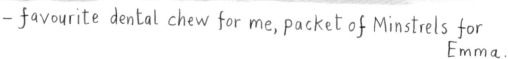

Wednesday 6th April

I have three new friends – Bartek, Marek, and Peter. Every day, they say "Good morning, Plum!" and then they paint the walls.

They are real artists, with big brushes and nice waistcoats,

but I am not allowed to "get in the way," so I have to sit with Emma while she dribs and drabs on scraps of paper and rubs things out, when all I want is to be with them.
I could so happily sit with them all day and watch paint dry.

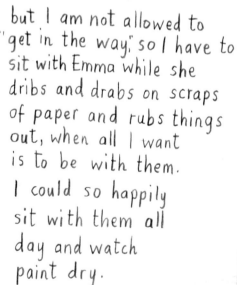

Saturday 9th April

My darling Rocket

came for
the afternoon.

Monday 11th April

Tee tum-tee-tum-tee-tum,
De-dum-de-dum-de-dum,
Tee-tooty-tooty-too too too
Diddle-um, diddle-um
Diddle-um . . .

Thursday 14th April

On just about the best walk
I've EVER been on, Beth and Duncan
and I agreed that we were very
glad we were DOGS, because if
you're a person - it's so
extremely important not to
get your feet wet.

Sunday 17th April

I have had quite a dreary week. Emma was working very hard all the time and the builders came and turned the whole house upside down. Then Emma had something done to her eye and spent a whole evening wailing and moaning and on top of all that - my daddy is away. I just have to remember "This too shall pass." I really hope so.

Wednesday 20th April

Fia →

Weezie ↙

I have had to do the blog all by myself today because Emma had an operation on her eye. First, I had to stay with Fia and Liffey. Then Weezie looked after us and then I came home. When Emma is better she will do the drawings again, but I think you might prefer mine.

Emma ↙

Saturday 23rd April

I am allowed to do one
more blog by myself with
my drawings.
I am in my favourite place.

It is sky and
sea and river and
marsh,

and Emma says I
smell like dead
frogspawn.
It's lovely, lovely,
lovely.

Monday 25th April

I have to admit
a lack of courage,
a loss of nerve,

a fearful dread
of things that BUZZ.

I do not like things that BUZZ.

My instincts are to take it lying down

So I retreat and am,
once again, defeated
by a belligerent
campaign of
hostile psychological
warfare.

Friday 29th April

I don't know how people manage without a Weezie in their lives.
She looked after me and she looked after Emma for ages.

She never moaned or groaned or rolled her eyes.

She is an angel without any wings.

I am going to buy her some in the Pound Shop, and a halo to wear in her lovely brown hair.

Sunday 1st May

Happy am I, the dog that swimmeth in the river the whole day long. I swimmeth upstream, downstream — wherever the tide taketh me...

... that is until cruel reality bites and the dream is over, replaced by the nagging presence of Emma and the extending lead.

Tuesday 3rd May

Jakey and I were dismayed to find Esther playing with a large ridiculous poodle this morning.

"She's OUR friend – NOT YOURS!" we said. "STOP IT, AT ONCE!"

But did they? They didn't even notice us.

"Pathetic!" said Jakey. "Pathetically childish!" I agreed.

Sunday 8th May

We had supper with Quentin and Linda. I know artists are supposed to be a bit vague because their minds are on higher things like books and pen nibs and chiaroscuro, but it would have been nice if, inbetween the astute observations and fascinating criticisms, anyone had remembered to give me something to eat. Not a sausage. Not even a crisp.

Monday 9th May

On our walk this morning I asked Esther what she does when Trisha is working. She said "I dream about swimming in a lake in Italy." While Emma was working I tried dreaming about swimming in the sea in Aldeburgh.

When I woke up I was still sitting in the same old chair and Emma was still working.

I spend my whole life WAITING, I thought. Waiting to swim. Then I fell asleep again and went swimming with Esther, in a lake in Italy.

Sunday 15th May

I saw Maisie last week. She said she was glad I'd come because she wanted to say goodbye.

She said that for a long time she'd been feeling very tired, and everything ached. I said, "Where you're going, will you feel better again?"

And she said, "I expect I'll feel marvellous all over!"
And she went, last Wednesday.
Dear Maisie. I hope she does
feel better now.

Wednesday 18th May

We stayed with my Dogfather, Sam. He paints and paints, whatever is in front of him. I sat right in front of him, hoping, but I just couldn't keep as still as the tulips. I would like to be painted properly for posterity so I asked Peg what she would do and...

...Peg said "Let's be kangaroos!"
So we were.

Sunday 22nd May   Liffey came to Suffolk and we went to the beach but it was barricaded off because of the Monsters who were playing a game of catch with boulders. We heard them crashing about all night and they were still there in the morning and now it's May and dogs aren't allowed on the beach till September. It seems Monsters are: well, live and let live, I suppose. Probably best not to go and upset them.

When Emma does her back exercises I try to encourage her and keep her moving.

She always looks as if she's about to give up.

I don't think she puts much effort into it,

certainly not as much as I do,

So I'm always glad when it's time to do the plank.

Sunday 29th May

Yesterday I met a man trying to teach his dog to dive into the river. She didn't have a clue.
"I'll show you! I'll show you!" I was thinking, but it wasn't my stick.

Then Emma brought a stick for me.
"Lucky dog," I thought, "for the chance to learn from a master."

Even in mid-air I could feel the charge of admiration from my little audience, mixed with a little dismay.

Wednesday 1st June

We went to see the birds in the park. They were having a lovely time, swimming, and being pleased with themselves- probably because dogs weren't allowed in. It was that sort of park. So I thought 'Stuff that!' and because I am a dog of resourceful spirit and dazzling originality, I found my own watering hole to stand in, without any birds in it.

We got stuck in the shed with Emma during a thunderstorm. Rocket and I were petrified—shaking like jellies, whereas Little Miss Liffey's face shone with pure demonic pleasure, the closer it got. The next day we went to Chiswick with Esther and found a huge swimming pool that had arrived overnight.

We went to see my publisher last week because they are making a little film about Moi. It is not just a walk-on part — I am the star. So now I am wondering — is my life going to change? Will I still be able to go about unmolested? Will my friends still love me for who I am? Can I have a continuous supply of chicken donuts from now on?

Saturday 11th June

Emma says
I have no
Empathy.
She's said
it before.

Of course I felt sorry for John Brown
with all his broken bones, and I tried to
show it on the way to his pool.
I am Emphatic when it comes to anything aquatic, but Emma says
Empathy and Emphatic are
NOT the same thing.

Sunday 12th June

My daddy loves his garden but he does not like slugs, so at night we go out and find them and then we despatch them.

Wednesday 15th June

Emma took me swimming on the island again. First I swam against the tide, then I swam with it, very, very fast. Then I did it all over again.

Emma is quite intelligent but sometimes her brain lets her down. It did it today. It should have calculated that as the water was coming in so very, very fast, we would be cut off. But it didn't...

"Oh no!" said Emma "Oh, Plum!" she said. "We're absolutely
stranded!" And we were. We'd have to act quickly.
"Am I bothered?" I thought... "hmmm, let me think..."
I had another lovely little swim and Emma's boots made
loud squelching noises all the way home.

Monday 20th June

In Suffolk, one of the first things
I do is visit Andy in the East Coast Cafe. I am a V.I.P. there
and they rely on my input. I don't get much input back though-not even a
croissant.

Saturday 25th June

I absolutely love my sister, Liffey, but we are completely different.

She doesn't like shingle beaches. She doesn't like swimming.

She is also a lap dog, which I am NOT, except when no one is looking.

Tuesday 28ᵀᴴ June   Liffey has gone home.

Even though she always sat in the front seat of the car,

and told me off constantly...

Even though she chewed up my favourite ball,

and insisted on sleeping in my bed...

Even though she stopped me going in the river when I wanted to and I came to the conclusion that sisters can be quite annoying..

...Liffey is MY sister-

my annoying sister, and I love her.

Thursday 30th June

I was so happy with my stick today.
Esther wanted it and that made me love it
even more. "A stick is a stick is a stick,"
I thought, and then Esther said I was being
annoying so I dropped it. Of course she picked it
up, so it became Esther's stick, and I had to adjust
all my feelings about it.

Saturday 2nd July

When we were walking by the river suddenly lots of little ducklings fell from the sky.

Their nest must have been on a high balcony.

They were very upset and they couldn't get over the wall to find their stupid mother who was waiting for them in the river. It was very worrying. We didn't know what to do... they were squeaking and running around. I was afraid another dog would catch them.

...then Emma decided: she dropped one over the wall into the water. First it went under and then it popped up again – and swam – for the first time! Then she dropped the rest of them, one by one, and they all swam away together. Phew!

I hope their stupid mother won't expect them to fly back up to the balcony again.

House of
Illustration →

Not sure
what is
behind
these
hoardings.

Monday
4th July
It was very exciting going
to Granary Square. First, we
saw my picture on the
hoardings, then the FOUNTAINS,
and then the brand new
House of Illustration and my friend,
Quentin's pictures* And then we
had **CROISSANTS** !
*They were quite good.

Friday 8th July

We went on the "sleeper" to Scotland. I think it should be called a WIDE AWAKER. I didn't sleep one wink because I had to be on guard. I could hear there were marauders outside. When we eventually got there Emma said she might have slept better "if she hadn't had SOMEONE's bony little elbows sticking into her all night."

Sunday 10th July
Check on Emma,
check the sea,
check Emma,
check the sea...

Wednesday 13th July
I don't actually swim a lot. I just stand here.
All day. Nothing actually happens. I don't expect it to.
Except people try to get me to come in, and I don't go.

Sunday 17th July

Emma says I am a weird dog. She doesn't know that I am entering for the Guinness Book of Records.

My record for standing in the sea is 4½ hours so far. She says that's why my paws are so sore, but I don't believe her,

Musher's Secret

and I feel stupid wearing rubber bootees.

She does everything she can to thwart me...

...they ALL do...

...which makes the challenge even more exciting...

...and the victory even more rewarding.

Tuesday 19th July

I went swimming in a bonny wee burn in the glen. It was bricht and blinterin, brattlin and braw. Och aye the noo. Toss me a caber Jimmy.

Friday 22nd July

My new thing in Scotland is pine cones. Emma has to collect them and throw them interestingly.

I capture them, one way or another.

It involves imagination, agility,

athleticism, accuracy—

a number of my natural talents,

not to mention spitting.

Monday 25th July We walked with Sally, Alex, Fin and Lily. Alex never wears shoes which proves that he is almost wild, like me, but he has to watch out for prickles. I wonder why humans didn't just get paws in the first place. They are so much better than feet.

<u>Friday 29th July</u> Today I don't know what to say. I've been thinking
and thinking but I haven't come up with anything so here is a picture
of what is on the other side of the woods here in Scotland.
It's freezing cold, by the way. Like winter. Nose-tingling. Arctic.

Monday 1st August

Back in London we visited Mike and Nellie. The river was very still and quiet and a flock of Canada geese were floating backwards with the tide. I think they were asleep.

Tuesday 2nd August

When I first met Mark's new dog, Clara, I was terrified. She had no idea how to make friends. Later, she told me about her tragic past. Some of it was too painful to speak of.
She doesn't even know about treats.

I realised that compared to Clara, I've led a charmed life. I've enjoyed a privileged upbringing, so I allowed her to lie in my Cath Kidston bed of roses for a while.

Wednesday 3rd August

When we got back to London it was freezing there too.
We went to the boring old park – at least I was expecting
it to be boring, but it wasn't, because my friends, Larry,
Jake and Bean were there. Generally I find that if I imagine
the worst I am happily surprised by how delightful
life can be.

Grandpa 1928-2016

Wednesday 17th August It's been a strange, sad time. Clara, Liffey, Maudie and I watched as they all walked down the road in their best clothes. Poor blind Maudie couldn't see, but I think she knew. I'm sure she knew.

Later on, we went
down to the church where
everything was still and quiet.
We looked at the pond on the other
side of the wall and a heron rose up
and flew away, into the pale evening sky.

Friday 19th August

This picture is Tuesday and the next one is Wednesday.
Emma says they are typical English summer weather—
poor old thing. Well, I love it. I'm indefatigable.
I'm effervescent. I'm tireless.
I'm YOUNG!

Saturday 20th August

We went to lunch with an unfeasibly large dog called Kilburn. My first thought was "HELP!"

But he was a creature entirely without malevolence and seemed rather in love with me, which had a shameful effect on my behaviour.

I've always believed in that old adage and had no qualms about using it - "Treat 'em mean to keep 'em keen"! And it absolutely, definitely, completely works.

Monday 22nd August

We were in Suffolk. It was glorious and heavenly. Every morning we had to go to Baggott's for a treat. All the dogs go. Then we walked with Helen and Peg. They were glorious and heavenly too. I swam in the sea, in ponds, in rivers, in ditches, but ...

...in the sea, I was the number one CHAMPION! No one could beat me—not even Helen. Peg was a witness.

My Dogfather, Sam Fogg, is a number one champion for bringing us here in the first place.

Wednesday 24th August Because of the rain, we had to wear our coats. Peg looked beautiful, as always, in hers. I looked and felt like a prat. But when we got to the boating pond all my desperate prayers were answered. Emma took my coat off and accidentally on purpose pushed me in.

Emma says I am very strong-willed. That's because I like to do everything my way, and I like it to be how I like it and I like to go where I want when I want.

But I've noticed that she is developing an iron will too.

Instead of waiting for me to come out of the sea when I feel like it — now she just walks away and the battle of wills is won...

... because she knows... she's finally realised, after all these years, that I NEVER, EVER WANT TO BE LEFT BEHIND !

Sunday 28th August

Well, we're all back - some of us by the skin of our teeth. When Esther had regaled us with stories of her travels through Italy and Monte carlo, Jakey described how in Spain he had been terrified by a sudden firework and had run off into the night. All alone, he ran.. he ran 5 kilometres through mountains and darkness, along roads he didn't know, and when he'd almost lost hope, after 4 hours of running - at last - he found his house.

Esther and I were moved to tears at this terrible vision, and the awful thought that we might, so easily, have lost, forever, our brave little friend.

Thursday 1st September

Rocket came over with a duck. A duck with a squeaker.

It had to be MINE.

So, after some gentle persuasion — it was. All mine.

But then, the Great Spoil Sport of Our Time arrived.

"I'm not going to let you unstuff Rocket's duck," she said, and confiscated it. What?! Life is totally UNFAIR. Why would she even think that?

Sunday
4th September

My daddy and
I have a new
toy. We
LOVE
it.

We just
LOVE
it.

We could play with
it all day long,
and sometimes
we do.

Monday 5th September

Esther can almost fit my whole head in her mouth.

I allow her to do it sometimes. I think it's good for her self-esteem, and to show my admiration for her I nuzzle her cheek, sweetly.

She always falls for it.

I reassert myself when she's least expecting it. The result is deeply satisfying every time.

Saturday 10th September

We met a little baby squirrel in the park. It was just sitting in the middle of the road, staring at us I think it had fallen out of a tree.

It tried to run up Emma's leg. Then it climbed into her hat. "Now what?" said Emma.

I hoped it wasn't coming home with us...

Emma put it in a tree in a woody place where it was safe, and then we walked away, very fast.

Monday 12th September

My friend, Boris, is a black labrador.

We have an affinity of spirit. I would say we were almost twins except he is tall and handsome, while I am petite with a certain je ne sais quoi.

We both know exactly what we want and exactly how to get it: we just gaze with our beautiful eyes...

...searing and irresistible.

<u>Thursday 15th September</u>

There are lots of apples in Grandma's garden. Emma throws them

and I pounce. They're one of my favourite things - versatile, delicious - like Grandma, except when she isn't. She didn't seem to like me jumping in the flowerbeds

and when I stopped she said, "Isn't it lovely and peaceful now that Plum's stopped whining?"

"Oh, Grandma," I thought. "Oh, Grandma. Grandma, Grandma."

Sunday 18th September

We've spent a lot of time in the car lately. It is utterly boring. Emma seems to forget I am even there.

She drives and drives, looking straight ahead, ignoring me, even when I moan. She listens to the radio.

So, I hide. Suddenly, she wonders where I am. She panics— convinced she left me behind somewhere, hours ago.

Then I pop up again. And on we go.

Wednesday 21st September

We ran away for three days.
I said to Emma
"Let's NOT go back."
But we always do.
Why? Why? Why?

Friday 23rd September

I often wonder about poor old Snooks. He sits by the boat pond and the bin, thinking, thinking. Does he remember why he is there? Does he remember the doctor and Dora? Is he thinking about them all the time? It's a nice place to be on a Summer's day, but how does it feel in Winter, all alone? and at his back the cold, cold sea.

Sunday 25ᵗʰ September

No one could say that I'm not an adaptable dog. One minute here—
the next, there. Gone are the empty shape-shifting skies, replaced
by squares of dirty grey. The distant crunch of shingled wave drowned
by roar and rush of car, and sweet dank smells of marsh and mist
erased by drain and urban fox...
FOX! Did somebody mention fox??
Ahh, London! My beating heart! Now I remember... forget the flipping
seagulls and the bloody flies... this is the proper place to catch a FOX!

Tuesday 27th September

In the middle of the night I heard those
dreadful foxes again and I leapt out of bed. Emma
usually gets cross about me barking and waking her
up but last night we looked out onto the street
and there was a fox cub all alone, standing
in the moonlight.

Wednesday 28th September

I was pleased that Emma persuaded my daddy to come for a walk, but we always forget that he doesn't much like walking...

... so he gets slower, and slower, and slower, and slower - until he's practically limping.

It's extremely tiring for me - having to keep running back to make sure he hasn't given up, or keeled over.

Sunday 2nd October

We were bowling along in a mad rush, as usual, about to get a parking ticket...

...when out of the corner of my eye, I suddenly saw something...

"Ta dah!" I said to myself "My day has finally come!" And Emma gaped, open-mouthed, lost for words, at last.

N.B. This is entirely a figment of Plum's imagination

Thursday 6th October

Some days are really hard work and I just CANNOT get Emma moving. It can take HOURS of concentration and dedication,

much patience and imagination...

but, usually, in the end, I BREAK HER!

Sunday 9th October

When I saw Esther today, I felt she was a little cool towards me and I realised I've been entirely self-obsessed lately. It's all been me, me, me. I completely forgot to say that in the Dog Show — she won 2nd prize for the Prettiest Bitch, and she was on TV. I would have given her 1st prize in all the categories, but it wasn't up to me.

<u>Monday 10th October</u> A funny thing happened when Weezie and Emma and I went to Gunnersbury.

They thought the pond had been emptied...

...but they were wrong. It had a lovely stinky pool in the middle,

and they couldn't get me out. They tried all the usual things, for AGES.

They even pretended to go home and leave me there...

…but I knew they were just hiding behind a tree.

Then a man came to help them and, suddenly, they sounded seriously cross so I had to give in.

Weezie had to throw away her shoes. I was in deep disgrace, so I suppose it wasn't such a funny thing after all.

At the weekend
I like to lie in –
for as long
as possible –

in their bed,
if possible,
especially if
they aren't in it
and I can really
stretch out properly.

They think I need
to be exercised all the
time but it's not true.
It's really not true.
I really like to LIE IN
at weekends if possible,
for as long as possible.
Really. I really, really do.

Saturday 15th October

Oh, Autumn. The one time when I am pleased with my coat - its blue so gorgeous with the million yellows, and I am looking glorious - not one of my friends is here to see me.

Tuesday 18th October

It was Emma's birthday this week and on the day we went to three parties. I wore a yellow ribbon for breakfast with the girls.

Then I wore a red one for Quentin's book launch where the French Ambassador made a speech.
After that we went to dinner with Other Emma and Johnny and I was immediately sick all over the carpet. Everybody said "Plum! Did you eat some of the French Ambassador's canapés?"
But I felt much too ill to think about it.

And then I was sick again.

Thursday 20th October

It was Emma *and* my daddy's birthday so we rented the Martello Tower for a week and some friends came to stay in it for a few nights each. Fia and Liffey stayed with us.

We had dinner in the tower every night and listened to the waves crashing on the shingle and I saw a ghost but nobody else did.

At the end of the week we were very tired so we went back to London for a good rest.

Saturday 22nd October
What I said about the tower was
actually really true: I saw a ghost—
well, definitely something.
I've never ever been
so scared.

Emma and my daddy were spooked too
so we went home and then Emma
googled "dog, shaking, crying, panting,"

and made an
appointment at the
vet to check me out.
He said it was
probably too much
leaping and jumping
and I might have
pulled a muscle or
slipped a disc, and it was pain that made me shriek... so no
more leaping. Unbelievable— NOBODY actually asked ME...

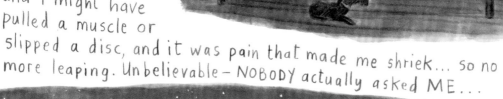

Sunday 23rd October

We went to Richmond Park with
Weezie, into the woods behind the wall.
I could smell bad foxes everywhere and
Weezie could smell autumn and chestnuts. When
we got home my daddy said he wished he could smell lunch.

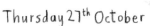

Thursday 27th October

On Saturday we were going to sign my book in Waterstones so I was very pleased that I had the chance to roll in the freshest and richest fox poo in the park, just before we left.

Of course, Emma didn't like it. She never does, but I knew others would be more appreciative, and I also knew that a bath wouldn't make much difference.

And I was right. All afternoon, the fragrant aroma of ripe fox poo wafted round the shop, and people congratulated me on my talents.

Sunday 30th October

My daddy went away today.
I think he will probably come back
because I've discovered, over the years, that
people usually do — but Emma and I both
felt absolutely bereft.

Tuesday 1st November

We've been having a quiet time, working, walking and playing while my daddy has been away. Emma has been cooking her sad little meals for one and in a daring break from tradition, she cooked spinach tonight.

But then she tipped it all over the floor. I am always eating off the floor so I said, "If the floor is good enough for me it's good enough for you too."

Obediently, she scraped it all up and ate it. "Good girl, Emma!" I said. "Very good girl!"

Friday 4th November

When Emma puts her coat on
my heart lifts.

When she puts her boots on
I am absolutely ready.

When she puts my lead on
I am buoyant and
optimistic,

until
I remember...

... that before we go ANYWHERE
there'll be at least three things
she's forgotten...

... and we'll
have to go
back to the
house... again,
again, and
again.

Saturday
6th November
I hardly dared believe the world would be
the same after all the dreadful, terrifying bangs and explosions
of last night. (I do not appreciate fireworks. I become a nervous WRECK.)
But there it was - glorious, smelly, dirty - unharmed and perfect, just
as it always was.

Monday 7th November

Last Monday...

...last Tuesday...

...and Wednesday...

...and Thursday.

But on Friday...

...on FRIDAY...

...he came HOME!

Tuesday 8th November

My cousin, Luca, knows as well as I do that there's absolutely no point in Adam saying "COME HERE, PLUM!"

Because I only ever do when I want to. That is how it is...

... but, in any case, Luca and I have better things to do,

and we do it over and over and over and over again.

Friday 11th November

The trouble with childhood friends is that they get bigger—

but they don't necessarily grow up. Nanook is a good example. When I see him I nod and hope he'll go away.

Despite being such a terribly "intelligent breed" he has NO idea about boundaries or personal space and I have to endure mortifying indignities.

Even my nastiest teeth-baring face has no effect. It seems to encourage him. What is it with blokes?

Tuesday 15th November

My darling Jakey was in the park this morning.

He's not only sweetly fragrant,

he's handsome, intelligent, charming...

...but then Larry arrived.

I'm secretly terribly in love with Larry. So very, very in love.

I hoped Jakey wouldn't notice. Oh, my! What a way to start the day.

Be still, my beating heart.

Friday 18th November Emma and Trisha were very sad when they saw all the trees that had fallen down in the storm along the river. They were so sad that they didn't even think of throwing any of the lovely sticks that were lying around, so Esther and I practised our Show Jumping instead.

Sunday 20th November

All my toys are wrecked and miserable.

This used to be a little piggy.

This was a really nice Christmas stocking.

This was a fantastic rubbery dinosaur.

I can't remember exactly what this was.

Emma says I must learn to look after them and stop taking their squeakers out, or I won't get any new ones —

and yet, she is the one who is prepared to be completely SAVAGE and RUTHLESS when it comes to tug-of-war.

Tuesday 22nd November
The day of the dreaded raincoat is here again.

Thursday 24th November

We went on a train to Sheffield to talk about my book. I could tell Emma was very nervous,

so I did my best not to let her down.

At the end, I had a chance to meet the audience, and I think it was then that Emma finally relaxed and realised that it wasn't all about HER.

Saturday 26th November

My cousins came and we walked along the river. When we got to the swimming place, nobody threw a stick. They just plodded past, each in their own little dream. Emma said, "Not today Plum. The current's so fast you'd end up in Henley!" Well, maybe I'd like it in Henley. People might notice me there.

Monday 28th November

I think squirrels are pointless and they have pea-sized brains.
I have a friend who catches them. I don't. Not because
they're too fast – it's really because I don't want
them to think that I even care.

Wednesday 30th November

I was very pleased to see my Uncle Mark and Sam and Grace, and, not so much - Clara. But, as often happens, I managed to put my feelings aside and put her first.

She had never been to London before.

So I explained all the smells to her and she was fascinated. "Here!" I said, "This must have been Rocket, about 20 minutes ago...

... and this was Rigby - and Larry, a bit earlier...

... and here's Sid, and Rocket again!" Clara was impressed.

"You have so many interesting friends, Plum," she said. "We only have sheep in Derbyshire."

Thursday 1st December

I found a perfect stick today. It was solid and dependable. It wasn't new – it had provenance. I could tell by the old toothmarks. It gave me a confident spring to my step and I carried it all the way home. When we got to my road, another dog came along and swiped it.

Sunday 4th December

We went to see Auntie-Emma's aunt, my great-aunt. I found it quite nerve-wracking because of the cat who is called Baby. I've never met anyone less like a baby. She is a complete bully, and last time I met her - she hit me!

It was one of the most mortifying experiences of my entire life.

Tuesday 6th December

We met a pathetic bear, dumped on the scrap heap of life. Is this really what happens to love? I wondered.

Emma picked him up and turned him over but he was still tragic, so we ended up carrying him down the road to the charity shop.

It hadn't opened yet so we left him sitting forlornly on the doorstep.

Maybe he'll get a second chance at love, I thought. Even an old bear who might not really be alive or have any real feelings deserves that.

Friday 9th December

Emma drove me to a meeting at my publisher. It wasn't very relaxing because of the traffic.

But when we got there, she was sweetness and light - even though no one was interested in her - only me and my ideas for my book.

I do have a lot of ideas, but I can't always remember what they are.

Sunday 11th December

Yesterday I felt desperate. The suitcase was in the hall, then the portfolio, then the bags. Am I going to be left behind? What happens if I'm left behind? I <u>am</u> going to be left behind, aren't I? Will I be all alone for ever and ever? The suitcase is going, and the bags and the portfolio, and Emma — and I will be left here... will I? Then Emma put my lead on me. Oh, my lead! Lovely lead!

"Come on, Tragedy Queen. Let's go!" she said, and we all left together, as usual.

Wednesday 14th December

We were by the sea again. Our friend Helen swims in it every day. We watch. There's certainly no chance that Emma or Peg would ever go in there - they only like looking at water - but I would. I would. I would. If it was a little bit warmer.

Friday 16th December

I love men. They are so adorable. It's not because they are clever. It's probably because they want to be so much— so when I am with them I know that the best way to make them happy is to let them think they are in control, so I am always a good girl and do as I am told.
I don't bother to do that with Emma.

Wednesday 21st December

We often stand on the steps and look at the river going by. Usually, there's nothing much to see - just river, and sometimes some ducks or a rude swan, but today... we saw Father Christmas. No sleigh, no reindeer, no presents - but definitely him. Probably on his way to the Pound Shop.

Sunday 25ᵗʰ December

It was a marvellous
Christmas. All the presents had to be
unwrapped so I got on with it -
lickety-split. Stalky and Brora
watched admiringly as I skilfully
shredded things. Only Rosie
seemed to have lost her Christmas
spirit - "It's meant to be about
sharing, Plum," she said. "It was
share and share alike in my day."
Well... I thought, but I didn't say -
that must have been a very, very
long time ago.

Grace   Sam

Ollie   Arthur   Tim

I had a really nice Christmas with my young relations. It was stress-free. I'm hoping that when Emma makes her New Year resolutions one of them will be to be less grumpy, but she'll probably forget.

Eliza   Anna   Kate
Rosie   Brora   Stalky

One of mine is to get more presents. It's my birthday in two weeks and two days. I hope she remembers this time.

Luca   Finn   Liffey   Will

Thursday 29th December Most mornings I aim to have some quiet time to myself after breakfast. It doesn't last long as the One With An Agenda of Ruthlessness and Iron Will cannot bear to relinquish control.

Saturday 31st December

My New Year Resolutions
① Be here now and always.
② Swim more.
③ Swim even more.
④ Catch a cat.
⑤ Catch a fox.
⑥ Spread Peace and Happiness to everyone (except cats and foxes)

1 3 5 7 9 10 8 6 4 2

Jonathan Cape, an imprint of Vintage Publishing,
20 Vauxhall Bridge Road,
London SW1V 2SA

Jonathan Cape is part of the Penguin Random House group of companies
whose addresses can be found at global.penguinrandomhouse.com.

The author acknowledges the kind permission of Liberty Ltd
to utilise the background artwork

First published in the United Kingdom by Jonathan Cape in 2017

penguin.co.uk/vintage

A CIP catalogue record for this book is available from the British Library

ISBN 9781911214274

Printed and bound in China by C&C Offset Printing Co., Ltd

Penguin Random House is committed to a sustainable future
for our business, our readers and our planet.
This book is made from Forest Stewardship Council® certified paper.

Pippin

Clara - my new aunt

Esther

Jake

Boris

Maudie - my aunt

Lily

Rosie   Stalky